Sleepover Girls is published by Capstone Young Readers
A Capstone Imprint
1710 Roe Crest Drive
North Mankato, Minnesota 56003
www.capstoneyoungreaders.com

Library of Congress Cataloging-in-Publication Data is available
on the Library of Congress website.
ISBN: 978-1-62370-194-9 (paperback)
ISBN: 978-1-4342-9756-3 (hard cover)
ISBN: 978-1-4342-9764-8 (eBook)

Summary: Delaney has always wanted a dog of her own, and she's
proving it to her parents by volunteering at the local animal shelter.
When the shelter enlists the Sleepover Girls to help with the annual
puppy fashion show fundraiser, the sleepover girls couldn't be more
excited (especially Delaney!). Delaney's parents even allow her to babysit
one of the dogs overnight during the weekly sleepover. But when the dog
gets lost, Delaney doesn't know what to do. Will the Sleepover Girls save
the puppy and Delaney's doggy dreams before the big fashion show?

Designed by Tracy McCabe

Illustrated by Paula Franco

Printed in China.
012015   008726R

sleepover Girls

DOG DAYS for

Delaney

by Jen Jones

capstone
young readers

Maren Melissa Taylor

Maren is what you'd call "personality-plus" —
sassy, bursting with energy, and always ready
with a sharp one-liner. She dreams of becoming
an actress or comedienne one day and moving
to Hollywood to make it big. Not one to fuss
over fashion, you'll often catch Maren wearing a
hoodie over a sports tee and jeans. She is an only
child, so she has adopted her friends as sisters.

Willow Marie Keys

Patient and kind, Willow is a wonderful
confidante and friend. (Just ask her twin,
Winston!) She is also a budding artist with
creativity for miles. She will definitely own
her own store one day, selling everything she
makes. Growing up in a hippie-esque family,
Willow acquired a Bohemian style that
perfectly suits her flower child within.

Delaney Ann Brand

Delaney's smart and motivated — and she's always on the go! Whether she's volunteering at the animal shelter or helping Maren with her homework, you can always count on Delaney. You'll usually spot low-maintenance Delaney in a ponytail and jeans (and don't forget her special charm bracelet, with unique charms to symbolize each one of the Sleepover Girls). She is a great role model for her younger sister, Gigi.

Ashley Francesca Maggio

Ashley is the baby of a lively Italian family. Her older siblings (Josie, Roman, Gino, and Matt) have taught her a lot, including how to get attention in such a big family, which Ashley has become a pro at. This fashionista-turned-blogger is on top of every style trend and shares it with the world via her blog, Magstar. Vivacious and mischievous, Ashley is rarely sighted without her beloved "purse puppy," Coco.

chapter One

I'm ready to shop pretty much *any* day of the week. I mean, what girl wouldn't be? But Saturdays at the mall are the absolute best. There's live music in the courtyard, good sales, and tons of people are wandering around (which makes for prime people-watching time). My BFFs Ashley, Maren, and Willow always have *tons* of good stories from our people-watching time together.

For as long as I could remember, Maren, Ashley, Willow, and I had been taking turns hosting sleepovers on Friday nights. The tradition had actually started kind of by accident, thanks to me and Maren.

See, Maren's mom works for a travel magazine. She goes on all kinds of cool trips. (Seriously, she's been everywhere — from Switzerland to South Carolina.) Because our moms are friends, my mom offered to watch Maren on shorter weekend trips so she wouldn't miss out on anything. Maren's parents are divorced, and her dad lives pretty far away. She stays with him when her mom was off globe trotting for longer periods of time.

One weekend, Maren invited me to sleep over to return the favor. Her mom said we could each invite one more person. I invited Ashley, Maren invited Willow, and the Sleepover Girls were born! We've been rotating houses ever since, and it's *always* an adventure. I really can't imagine my life without my Sleepover Girls!

Anyway, back to the *real* reason I'm addicted to Sunday shopping. Every Sunday the local animal shelter has its pet adoptions in the parking lot. Every week, they bring a bunch of dogs and cats that need homes. It's so much fun petting and playing with the animals. I guess it's the second-best thing to actually *having* a dog, which I'm determined to do someday. Sadly, I have yet to convince my parents of this, no matter how hard I try.

"You guys, I'm obsessed with this dress," said Ashley. She twirled out of the dressing room wearing a purple print maxi dress. "It was meant to be mine, right?"

Willow picked at the price tag. Her eyes got wide. "Um, more like meant to be a millionaire's! This thing is, like, $350," she said. "I bet I could find some fabric at the store and make you something just as cool." Willow was crazy-artsy. It seemed like there was nothing she couldn't do with a paintbrush or pair of scissors in hand — including sewing.

Ash looked in the mirror, smoothing the sides of the dress wistfully. "I might take you up on that," she said. "Can we at least take a pic for the blog?"

I whipped out my phone to snap a pic, and chose a cool filter effect to make the colors pop even more. "Consider yourself Instagrammed," I told her.

Ashley had just started a Tumblr page centered around fashion called "Magstar." (Her last name is Maggio.) Her blog had actually gotten a pretty good following so far. I wondered how many "likes" and reblogs this one would get. Maybe Ash would even give me a shout-out for shooting the photo. I could see the hashtag now: *#laneybehindthelens*

Clearly bored, Maren grabbed an over-the-top fake fur coat from a nearby rack. "What about this one?" she said, pursing her lips to make a duck face, or as a I call it, the "selfie" face. "Am I top-model material or what?"

The idea of Maren modeling was pretty much unthinkable. She rarely strayed from her "uniform" of hoodie, jeans, and some sort of sports T-shirt. Today it was a Cleveland Browns tank top, which looked adorably ridiculous under the fur coat.

"Okay, that's it," I said. "Maren's going crazy, and I think we're officially over shopping for clothes. Can we *please* go see the dogs now?" Willow nodded in excitement, and I knew Ashley would be game. She was a big dog lover, too, and even had one herself. (Lucky girl!) So once Ashley got changed and reluctantly let go of her latest fashion find, we headed outside to check out the dog adoption.

"Sunlight!" joked Maren, shielding her eyes from the bright light. "Ashley was in the dressing room for so long I forgot what daylight looked like."

Ash took pity and handed Maren her oversized sunglasses. "Here," she said. "You need them more than I do." Maren wearing Ashley's glam sunglasses with her sporty tank top looked totally out of place, and we all dissolved into fits of laughter again.

We finally made it out to the parking lot, where pets and people were gathered under some shady trees. A large banner read "Valley View Pet Rescue." About fifteen dogs were playing and hanging out inside a really big, round open cage. My heart immediately melted, which happens every time I see dogs from the shelter.

"Oh look!" said Willow, pointing at a sweet-looking yellow Labrador retriever. "Delaney, meet my new best friend." I could see why she'd noticed him right away. He seemed to be smiling, with his tongue hanging out. His floppy ears were so precious!

"He *is* a lovebug, isn't he?" Maren said as she petted his head gently. He began nuzzling her arm. Labs definitely seemed to be one of the gentlest breeds. He would clearly make a good companion.

"Oh my goodness! Look at this little muffin," said Ashley, running over to say hi to a fluffy white Maltese with a pink bow in its fur.

"You already *have* a purse dog," teased Maren. Ashley's dog Coco (who was named after famous designer Coco Chanel) was a pint-sized chihuahua who often traveled with Ash in her purse. I blamed it on her reading too many celebrity gossip magazines. Ash loved following in the fashionable footsteps of her fave starlets, all of whom seemed to love parading their pets in the pages of *Teen Vogue*. At least those pets had homes, even if they were treated as accessories.

Ashley petted her huge yellow handbag with a grin. "I always have room for more," she laughed. "Better yet, I could buy another purse!" We all laughed at that.

Ashley leaned over the cage to pick up the fluffball. "Aren't *you* a cutie?" she cooed, rubbing her nose against the dog's. "You'd love to be my purse pal, wouldn't you? Oh yes, you would . . ."

Growl! The dog snapped at Ashley, showing its teeth and hissing. One of the older volunteers rushed over to us and grabbed the dog from a scared Ashley's clutches.

"You should never pick up a dog without asking!" she scolded. She started petting the dog to try to calm it down and quickly walked away from us.

Then it happened. I saw *my* dream dog. Sitting quietly in the corner, he looked like a mini version of Lassie. A little boy was petting him, and he was just sitting there patiently. He was the sweetest thing ever! As far as I was concerned, it was definitely love at first sight. Now I just had to figure out how to make him mine.

chapter Two

"So you're a fan of Frisco, I see!" A volunteer scooped up my Lassie look-alike and brought him over to us. Up close, Frisco was even harder to resist. He had the pointiest nose and big brown eyes. His long fur was different shades of tan, brown, and gold. He even had a little lion's mane around his head. I really couldn't take the cuteness factor. It was completely off the charts!

"Aww, Frisco! Can I hold him?" I asked. She happily handed him over to me. He squirmed a little, then laid his head against my chest once he got comfy. Frisco was definitely heavier than I'd thought!

"He's about fifteen pounds," said the volunteer, reading my mind. "He's a Sheltie, or a Shetland Sheepdog."

Ashley reached out tentatively to pet Frisco, and he offered his paw in return. She shook it with a relieved smile. "I guess not *all* of them woke up on the wrong side of the dog bed," she said, shooting the white fluffball a joking glare.

The fluffball didn't seem to mind. She just gave Ashley a little scowl and turned the other way. I couldn't imagine that anyone was going to adopt that little dog!

The volunteer, whose name tag read "Skylar," ruffled Frisco's fur affectionately. She gave me a look of approval.

"Frisco gets along with everybody," she said. "And you two seem to be getting along famously. Any interest in giving him a good home? He's living at the shelter right now and would make a wonderful new friend."

The idea of little Frisco stuck in an animal shelter with lots of homeless dogs made me so sad. Of course I would have loved to rescue him! (File that under "duh.") But before I could respond, Willow spoke up. "Delaney's parents won't let her have a dog," she told Skylar. "That's why she makes us come to these adoptions every week. Seriously. She comes every single week."

"I knew you looked familiar. I apologize for not introducing myself to you earlier," Skylar said. "These events are always busy, which is a good thing. However, that doesn't leave me much time to walk around and talk to everyone who shows up."

"That's okay," I replied. "The important thing is to get these dogs into good homes."

"Isn't that the truth," Skylar replied.

Ashley piped in. "You should see Delaney when we go to the pet store. She goes crazy! When she came with me to get my baby, Coco, I practically had to drag her out when it was time to leave!"

Skylar frowned. "I'm glad you found a pet you love, but can I ask why you went to the pet store instead of a shelter? We always have so many animals that need good homes," she said.

"I'm not really sure. Now I just feel bad," Ashley said.

"Oh, no!" Skylar said. "Don't feel bad. Just remember other options when you get your next pet, okay?"

I felt a little embarrassed for Ashley. I decided to change the subject. "Well, what's Frisco's story?" I asked.

Skylar explained how Frisco and his brothers had been found in an abandoned house in a bad area. They'd had no food or water for days. Thankfully, the rescue had been able to nurse them back to health.

"We've found new families for all of the dogs in the litter except for Frisco," explained Skylar. "So you can see why he needs a good home! Are you *sure* your parents won't come around?"

I shook my head. "I doubt it," I told her. "I've been trying to convince them for as long as I can remember. They don't have time to take care of a dog, and they think I'm too young to handle the responsibility. They barely trust me to babysit my little sister, and she's just two years younger than I am."

What I *didn't* say was that I'd much rather take care of a dog than watch my younger sister, Gigi. Don't get me wrong — I love my little sister to death, but she could be a real handful sometimes. I guess that's just part of having a younger sister, right?

"Well, we can always use good volunteers here at the rescue," Skylar said. "Why don't you start helping us out? Maybe that would show your parents how serious you are about it. Plus, you could spend lots of time with Frisco."

Frisco barked, as if to agree. It was a light-bulb moment, for sure! Why hadn't I thought of that sooner? Skylar was a genius.

"Count me in," I told her. "I'll ask my parents about it and hopefully I can start next weekend. This is a dream come true."

"It would be great timing," said Skylar. "We have a doggy fashion show fundraiser coming up, and we need all the help we can get. Maybe your friends can even help us out, too."

Skylar gave us more information on the doggie fashion show fundraiser. This seemed like the perfect event for the sleepover girls!

Ashley's eyes lit up. The words "fashion show" were all she needed to get on board. And Maren seemed to like the idea, too. She grabbed a nearby stick and started using it like a fake microphone. "I know a great MC if you need one," she said. "I'll even do it for free!"

It's funny — all of my friends are so different. Maren was always hamming it up. That girl was born to be onstage. Doggie fashion show today, Hollywood starlet tomorrow. In fact, her love of performing was actually a big reason why we had become friends. Our moms had put both of us in the same musical theatre class when we were 5 years old. In the play at the end of the class, Maren played the lead of Orphan Annie. Oh, and I guess who I played? The dog, Sandy. This would probably be a nightmare for most girls, but playing a dog was perfect for me. To this day it's one of my best memories, and the pictures are priceless!

Willow is a true artist. She could probably make a beautiful sculpture out of a paper bag! Seriously, I'm 100 percent sure she'll have her own shop one day. She's always making jewelry and other cool crafts. Today, she was wearing a paper mâché bead necklace she'd made out of old maps. (Needless to say, birthday gifts from her are awesome.) And she looks exactly how her name sounds. She's super-tall, slender, and has really pale blond hair and green eyes.

As for Ashley, she's one-of-a-kind, too. She comes from a really loud Italian family, so she's not afraid to speak her mind. Thanks to them, she also knows how to make one mean plate of pasta! And one look at her closet (or Tumblr) leaves no doubt that the girl has a serious passion for fashion. She knows every designer and then some! But beyond that, she's one of the bravest, most awesome people I know. I've known her the longest out of anyone. When school frazzles me, I can always count on her to set me straight.

Now I just needed to add a new four-legged friend to the mix, and my life would be complete! And being Valley View Rescue's newest volunteer was getting me one step closer to making that happen for real . . . or so I hoped.

chapter Three

The next morning, I decided to wear my special charm bracelet to school. Maren had gotten it for me for my birthday last year. I wore it whenever I needed a little luck, and today I needed some luck. Part of what makes it so special to me is that four of the charms represent my friends and me. The paint palette is a symbol for Willow; the drama mask is for Maren; the pair of kissy lips is for Ashley; and mine, of course, is a dog bone.

I was putting on some lip gloss in the mirror when my sister Gigi leaned over my shoulder. "Ooh, cool, honey-flavored," she said, reading the label. She grabbed the gloss out of my hand. "Let me try! Please? Please? Please?"

"You wish!" I told her. I swiped it back. "Mom wouldn't let me wear lip gloss until sixth grade, so you'll have to wait your turn, too."

Gigi was only in fourth grade. Plus, I felt way more grown up than her now that we went to different schools. I was in the middle school, and she was still stuck at the elementary. *Sayonara*, sis!

"Delaney, do you want a baloney sandwich or a veggie pita?" called my dad from the kitchen, where he was getting our lunches ready.

"Whatever's easier for you, Dad," I replied. It couldn't hurt to kiss up a bit! I'd talked to my parents last night about helping out at the shelter. After a bit of back and forth, they'd said yes. The only condition was that I still had to get my schoolwork done on the weekends, too. Easy peasy, right? I figured I might as well keep the good vibes going and see if I could sway them. Operation Frisco was in full effect! (They didn't know that part of it, of course.)

As usual, Ashley was waiting by my locker that morning after homeroom. We always walked to social studies together so we could catch up a little before class. It's amazing how much we have to talk about even though we see each other every day and talk most nights.

Can I just say that having a locker is one of the coolest things about going to the middle school? (Second only to the iPads they give all of us students!) Willow helped me decorate the inside of my locker with some fake wallpaper. I'd also hung up a few pics of my friends and I using funky-shaped magnets. There was a photo of us at the zoo field trip last year, a slumber party pic of all of us in sleeping bags, and a photo booth strip of me and Ash making funny faces. Ash had pulled the entire locker together with a little chandelier. She gave each one of the sleepover girls one before school started. All in all, my locker looked pretty darn amazing, if I do say so myself. Maybe Ashley would feature it in a "Lockers You Wish You Had" post on her Magstar blog.

"How'd it go with the parentals last night?" asked Ashley. Today she was wearing floral-rimmed reading glasses and the perfect summer dress with a light-weight cardigan over it. Her hair was up in a loose topknot bun. She always looked effortlessly chic. Personally, I'm fine in a ponytail and jeans, but I give her tons of fashionista cred for showing up to school in style every day.

"Pretty good," I answered her, grabbing my social studies textbook and slamming my locker shut. "You're looking at Valley View Rescue's newest volunteer!"

Ashley high-fived me, almost dropping her own armful of books in the process. *"Bueno!"* she exclaimed. "Let the dog days begin."

I smiled and rubbed my dog bone charm. It was turning out to be a pretty good week! That was, *until* I got to social studies class, when Mr. Costa made an unwelcome announcement.

"I trust you all did the required reading over the weekend on the ancient Mayans," he said. "And now you get to prove it. It's pop quiz time! Go ahead and put away everything except your iPads and sign into Blackboard."

My heart sunk. I'd totally forgotten to do the reading last night in all of my excitement over Frisco and working with the rescue. Instead, I'd spent all night on Petfinder. I wanted to be well-informed when I started to volunteer, and looking at dog pics and reading up on the different breeds was so addictive. Oops. Hopefully I knew enough about pyramids and predictions to get me through. Fake it 'til you make it, right?

I shot Ashley a look, but she was already face-down in her iPad. That girl was a rock star when it came to social studies. I was more of a math and science girl, myself. I rubbed my charm again for good luck, then got down to business.

I did the best I could, but I didn't know a lot of the answers (I doubt many people know about pyramids and predictions unless you actually study it, so this was not easy.) I tried to make educated guesses and got through the quiz pretty quickly. There was no point dragging it out when I really had no idea what the answers were.

Oh well, I thought as I pressed "submit." The results? 10/15. Not great, but probably a little better than I deserved. Note to self — better buckle down next weekend or my days as a volunteer at the rescue were over before they even started! I was disappointed in myself, but I knew my parents were going to be even more disappointed. This was definitely a step back in Operation Frisco.

As I was waiting for everyone else to finish the exam, I signed into my messenger. Our teachers didn't love it when we did this during class, but I really needed a morale boost after my bad quiz. Almost immediately after signing on, a note from Maren popped up.

RedheadsRock: Is it 3:00 yet?

I stifled a giggle. Maren had ADHD, so she was always getting bored in class. Translation: lots of IMs from her! I quickly typed back.

LaneyforLife: Not even close. I'm having a quiz meltdown over here.

RedheadsRock: Oh no! What's up?

Forgetting to do the assigned reading is not a good start to my week or impress my parents.

RedheadsRock: Uh-oh. I'll bring you a Red Vine afterward to make it all better.

LaneyforLife: Red Vines sound divine! What's new in your world?

RedheadsRock: Not much. Chase Davis keeps throwing little paper wads at me when Ms. Long isn't looking. He is so immature!

LaneyforLife: You know you love it!

RedheadsRock: I do not! I don't need some stupid boy taking up my precious time.

LaneyforLife: Okay, okay. Calm down. I was only joking!

Unlike me, Willow, and Ashley, Maren wasn't interested in dating yet. (Not that any of us could actually go on dates, but it was fun to have a new crush every so often.) Chase was one of the cutest guys in our grade. Of course he would like the one person who could care less. Chase had confidence for miles, so I'm sure he won't just give up. It makes me smile just knowing that Maren was annoyed by something that the rest of us would have liked. Classic, Maren!

Mr. Costa's timer rang, so I typed a quick goodbye to Maren. We still had about fifteen minutes left, and I couldn't afford to miss a minute. I turned my attention to Mr. Costa for the rest of class, taking furious notes. No more so-so grades for this girl! I had a puppy to adopt, after all!

chapter Four

Friday is the greatest day ever! I know, I know. EVERYONE loves Fridays. But I have an extra good reason to love Fridays (besides our weekly sleepovers, obviously). After school, I was going to take a tour of the Valley View Animal Shelter and get a little volunteer training. I couldn't wait to see Frisco again! Willow offered to come with me and my mom, since the Tae Kwon Do class she usually takes after school was canceled.

I managed to make it through the school day, though I got pretty squirmy near the end. By the time my mom picked me and Willow up, I was ready to burst! As it turned out, the shelter was a lot bigger than I'd pictured. It had a really cool mural painted on the side wall showing pets with happy families. (I bet Willow could have added a finishing touch or two!) As if she'd read my mind, Willow said, "Is that a Romero Britto mural? I love it!" Only Willow would be able to pinpoint the artist just by looking at it.

Inside the lobby, the same woman who'd introduced us to Frisco was sitting behind the front desk. "I wasn't sure you guys would come back," she joked as we approached. "I'm glad you decided to do this. And this must be your mom." She reached out to shake my mom's hand. "I'm Skylar."

"Hi, I'm Maureen," said my mom, offering her hand in return. We could hear lots of loud barks and howls coming from inside the shelter, and I could tell my mom felt a little bit out of place. My parents weren't really "pet people." My mom knew how much it meant to me though, and she gave my a shoulder a little squeeze. "Delaney is so excited to be getting involved here. Thanks for having her," she added.

Skylar smiled. "Well, we need people of all ages helping out, and we're excited to have Delaney on board! Let me find someone to cover the desk, and I'll take you on a tour," she offered. "Oh, and yes, you'll get to see Frisco." My mom raised her eyebrows and shot me a look. She probably knew my wheels were turning!

Once we were inside the shelter, my good mood started to go south. The kennel was this really long hallway. Lots of stalls sat right next to each other, with up to five dogs in each one. The stalls were mostly clean, but the area was still pretty smelly. Some of the dogs were sleeping, and others were sitting sadly in a corner. But lots of them came eagerly trotting up to the front of the stall as soon as they saw us, wanting to be petted or given treats. It was so sad to see them behind the bars! I hated knowing they were stuck here, waiting and hoping for someone to adopt them.

One look at Willow's face told me she felt the same way. "What happens if they don't get adopted?" she asked, looking worried.

"Well, at some shelters, they actually have to put the animals to sleep because of overcrowding," Skylar answered. Seeing my horrified look, she quickly put us at ease. "This is a no-kill shelter, thankfully, which means we keep the pets till they find a good home. That's why the adoptions are so important — so that it doesn't turn into a zoo in here!"

As we walked down the hallway, Skylar introduced us to some of her favorite dogs, which cheered me up. There was Chicken, one of the strangest-looking dogs on the planet. He was mostly hairless except for a big chunk of hair sticking straight up from his head! Then there was Miley, a caramel-colored standard poodle whose elderly owner had just passed away. And Dig-Dug the Pug, a wrinkly ball of love that Willow went crazy over.

"Oh, Win would love Dig-Dug," Willow said, bending down to pet Dig-Dug. "Win" was her fraternal twin, Winston. "He's been obsessed with pugs ever since he saw that movie *Milo and Otis* when we were younger."

I could relate. *Lady and the Tramp* had been the movie that had sparked my own obsession with dogs, followed closely by *Beverly Hills Chihuahua.*

Then, in the best stall of all, I saw my own real–life star, Mr. Frisco! I may have been imagining it, but he seemed excited to see me.

I swear we had a connection already. One of the volunteers had tied a red scarf around his neck, so he looked like a little cowboy. "Howdy, partner!" I said in my best cowboy accent, sticking my hand between the bars so I could pet his head.

Skylar opened the stall door to let him out so that Willow and I could play with him a little bit. Frisco quickly ran toward me and hopped up, putting his front paws on my thigh. My smile couldn't get any bigger at this point. I dangled one of the treats Skylar had given us in the air.

"Sit, Frisco," I said with authority. He quickly sat down, his tongue hanging out in anticipation. We already make a great team! I handed him the treat as a reward. After he ate it, he started running in circles excitedly. It was beyond adorable! Even my mom had to smile at the sight of him.

"Mom, isn't Frisco the best?" I asked.

"And let me guess. You want Frisco to come home with us," she said. "I think we both know your dad isn't going to go for that."

Skylar stepped in. "You could always consider fostering a dog and see how that goes," she said. She began telling us all about the need for foster homes and how they help place dogs until they find a permanent family. I mouthed a silent "thank you" to Skylar for helping me plant the seed!

It was tough to say bye to Frisco, but we had to take the rest of the tour. Skylar really took us behind-the-scenes! She showed us the medical exam rooms where the vets help injured or sick animals. We also got to see the exercise yard, where the animals run, play, and let off a little steam. There was the cat area, with lots of cages stacked up against the wall. (Willow got a little sneezy because she's super-allergic to cats.) And the food prep room was pretty insane. I'd never seen so much pet food! It was quite an operation they had going on here.

We came to another room, which was basically a closet with a lot of old comforters in it. "We're always in desperate need of old blankets and bedding so that the pets can sleep more comfortably," Skylar explained. "If you've got anything lying around at home, we'd love to have it."

My mom looked thoughtful. "I'm sure we can dig up some donations," she said, smiling my way. Promising development! Maybe I'd convince my parents yet.

Once we finally got back to the lobby, Willow noticed a poster on the wall that read, "Annual Valley View Rescue Fashion Show Fundraiser!" The poster had tons of pictures of dogs in fun costumes, strutting down the runway with volunteers. The pictures were too adorable for words.

"Is this that event you told us about last week?" Willow asked Skylar.

"It sure is. Did you guys have time to look over the information I gave you on Saturday? I was serious about getting you girls involved," said Skylar.

"We did, but we aren't sure what we can do to help," I explained. "We don't have much time to raise money since it's next week already."

"I have the perfect solution!" Skylar said. "How would you and your friends like to be models in the show? We could use some young, fresh energy!"

Willow and I looked at each other excitedly. "Count us in!"

Skylar filled us in on what we would need to do. Willow looked pretty excited, and I couldn't wait to tell the other girls all about it at the sleepover tonight!

chapter Five

It was Ashley's turn to host the sleepover this week. Her house is always a loud and lively place because she has four siblings. Add the three of us to the mix and things get even more chaotic, which is amazing.

Sure enough, the night had already brought some craziness. A giant rainstorm had started while Willow and I were riding our bikes over to Ashley's. The result? Soggy sleeping bags — and even soggier sleepover girls! Luckily, Ashley's mom helped us warm up with some hot chocolate while she cooked an amazing spaghetti dinner, complete with turkey meatballs (which just happen to be my favorite). Going to Ashley's was like going to a real Italian restaurant, and I loved it!

"Why don't you girls go finish drying off while Ashley helps me with the sauce?" said Ashley's mom, giving her a pointed look. Ashley rolled her eyes, then curtsied and held out the sides of her frilly pink apron. She was a reluctant cook, but at least she looked good doing it.

"Your wish is my command, Mother," Ashley said with a smile.

"Very funny," her mom replied. "Now start stirring, young lady."

Soon we were all around the dinner table, slightly drier and definitely ready to eat. It was us four girls, plus Mr. and Mrs. Maggio and Ashley's older sibs Gino, Matt, and Roman. Her sister, Josie, was already in college, so she was off doing the whole college thing. I wasn't sure how Ashley remained such a girly girl with all of these guys around all of the time, but at least she got extra attention being the only girl at home. We all know she loved that! Plus, when Josie did come home for a visit, Ashley could grill her on college life.

And, of course, who could forget Coco? She was stationed under the table begging for some garlic bread. She, too, was a little soggy since Ashley had taken her for a short walk before we got here and also got caught in the rain storm. Somehow Ashley still looked perfect, even with wet hair. I don't know how she does it!

"So, Delaney, Ashley tells me all of you are going to be in a fashion show for the animal shelter," said Mr. Maggio, heaping a spoonful of spaghetti onto a dish and handing it to me. "Is this event open to the public? We'd love to come support it."

"Oh yes, definitely," I said between bites. "It's actually a fundraiser, so the more people who come the better! Ten dollars gets you in the door, and there will also be a raffle with really cool prizes."

Ashley's brother Gino laughed. "Can we put Coco up for auction? I'm sure some other family would *love* to listen to her bark all of the time," he joked. Ashley swiftly kicked him under the table, and as if on cue, Coco let out a few loud barks.

After dinner, we all set up our stuff in the basement, which was ground zero for our sleepovers at Ashley's. Her parents had set it up like a game room, with a giant big-screen TV, some old vintage pinball games, beanbags, and sports posters everywhere. There was also an old jukebox, which Ashley wasted no time turning on. She grabbed her latest issue of *Teen Vogue* and danced over to where we were laying out our sleeping bags.

"Let's do each other's hair," said Ashley. "I saw this really cool beachy wave look in *Teen Vogue* that I want to try out." She dangled the issue in the air with a grin.

Willow and I were game, but Maren wrinkled her nose in response. "I'm so not feeling the hairstyle thing," said Maren. "My hair need some TLC, not more experiments. Remember what happened last time I let you do my hair?"

"It was just one bad dye job," huffed Ashley, flopping down onto her fancy sleeping bag.

None of us could forget when Ashley dyed Maren's hair for Halloween. Maren's gorgeous red hair was supposed to be turn one shade darker and wash out after ten shampoos. Instead, it turned a deep purple and wouldn't wash out. Needless to say, Maren has been pretty protective of her hair ever since.

She started grooming Coco's fur. "Well, let's play 'Would You Rather?' then."

Now *that* was something we could all agree on. "Would You Rather?" was one of our favorite sleepover traditions, along with sunset bike rides, and DIY spa treatments. We always got a little bit outrageous with our questions, and we *always* learned something new about each other (I have no idea how anyone has any secrets anymore!).

Maren got to go first. "Delaney," she said, turning toward me. "Would you rather . . . be stuck in a jail cell with Franny and Zoey forever or live in a cage at the animal shelter?"

I almost spit out my soda at that one. Franny and Zoey, aka the "Prickly Pair," were not only twins, but also the mean girls in our class (they aren't always mean, but it's not easy to shed that image.) Spending a lifetime in jail with them would probably be worse than the death penalty!

"Animal shelter, definitely," I answered. "At least I'd get to hang out with the animals 24/7! Okay, my turn to go. Willow, would you rather be a werewolf or a zombie?"

Willow looked up from the friendship bracelet she'd started braiding on her knee. "I'm gonna have to go with zombie," she said. "Being a werewolf would involve way too much hair. It would be hot, itchy, and too much work. I don't have time for all of that shaving!"

Maren let out a long howl, causing us all to howl with laughter — both at Maren's silliness and the mental picture of Willow as a real-life teen wolf.

"Okay, Ash, it's all you," said Willow. "Think about it: would you rather be two feet tall or seven feet tall?"

Ashley looked deep in thought. "That's a toughie," she said. "If I was two feet tall, I'd be like a cute little fairy Thumbelina. But at seven feet tall, I could be the tallest international supermodel and work the runway without even wearing heels. Seven feet tall it is!"

The thought of an Amazon-sized Ashley working it supermodel-style wasn't even remotely weird. She could definitely hold her own, no matter what height she was! And she was pretty good at coming up with "WYR" questions, too.

"Maren, your turn," said Ashley. "Would you rather kiss Chase Davis or kiss a slimy frog?"

"Do I *have* to choose?" Maren groaned. She knew the answer to that — anyone who refused to answer a question was forced to give everyone a pedicure and manicure.

"I guess Chase Davis, but he wins only by a slim margin." Maybe she was finally coming around to the boy-crazy side after all! Now that would be a new development worth talking about.

"I know who you *really* want to kiss," said Ashley, flipping her *Teen Vogue* open to an article about Luke Lewis. "Lukey-loo!"

Luke Lewis was this really hot pop star who had actually grown up in our hometown. He was like royalty around here, and Maren was a certified super-fan. Her entire bedroom was covered with posters of him!

Maren swatted Ashley with her pillow, but then broke down laughing. "Okay, you're right," she admitted. "But can you blame me?" She had a point. Love or hate his music, Luke was a total hottie!

A few more rounds of "Would You Rather?" and we were ready to move on to something different. And Willow had just the plan. "Let's go raid the fridge!" she said, rubbing her belly. "I'm starving." Willow had a bottomless stomach, which was impressive and a little scary. I've never seen such a thin girl eat so much in my life!

"Seriously?" I asked. "I'm still stuffed from the spaghetti!"

Ashley sat up. "Actually, my mom *did* bake a tray of brownies for us earlier today. I totally forgot about them!" Even I had to admit that sounded yummy. (Who can't make room for freshly baked brownies?)

"What are we waiting for?" Willow asked. "Brownie time!"

We snuck upstairs to raid the refrigerator, or in this case, the brownie tray. We also popped some popcorn, so we could take part in another sleepover tradition — a scary movie! But Maren had another brilliant idea in mind.

"Look what I found," she said, whipping a DVD out of her bag. "Our old talent show video!"

"No *way*," said Ash, grabbing it away from her. "The one where Franny and Zoey did that weird mirrored dance?'"

"You know it," said Maren, giggling. And as we watched the ancient vid, I couldn't help but get a little sentimental. I really was thankful for my friends.

chapter Six

The sleepover fun usually continues well into Saturday morning. First on the agenda was homemade French toast, courtesy of Ashley's mom. I told you, she is an incredible cook. Of course, we were a little groggy from staying up late, so after breakfast, we all took Coco on a long walk around the neighborhood. *She* certainly had no shortage of energy in the morning! It was fun to picture what walking Frisco every morning would be like.

I didn't have too long to lounge around at Ashley's house, though. Duty called — I had to work my first pet adoption today. My directions were to report to the mall at 10:30 a.m. sharp. I was super-excited to make my debut as a volunteer! Even cooler? The girls were coming with me to meet their fashion show "buddies" and later, we'd all go shopping for outfits together.

"Hey girls!" Skylar greeted us as we approached the adoption area in the mall parking lot. "You're just in time to help set up. I didn't expect all of you to help, but the more the merrier!"

I glanced at the girls to see if they were willing to help. After all, they weren't the ones volunteering their time, so I didn't want them to feel like they had to. (After all, Ashley didn't usually like anything that cut into her valuable shopping time!) But the girls looked happy to help out, so I wasn't going to argue. Willow and Maren pitched in by unloading the cat carriers from the van. Ashley and I helped a few of the other volunteers, who were setting up the portable play area for the dogs.

Once everything was set up, Skylar came over to us with her clipboard. "We still have a few minutes before it's time for the adoption event to start, so I wanted to give you the rundown on your model mutts for the fundraiser," she said.

"This is where it gets fun," Ashley said.

"It sure does. Maren, you're going to be rocking the runway with Dig-Dug the Pug!" Skylar said with a smile.

At the mention of his name, Dig-Dug perked his ears, then grunted a little bit. He and Maren would make a really cute couple, especially since they were going to go with a caveman theme. Maren was a perfect Pebbles Flintstone type with her bright red hair. Just add a dog bone, and she was a shoo-in for the classic cartoon cutie.

Willow got her match — Hunter, the yellow Lab she'd hit it off with at last week's adoption. They seemed to be made for each other, too. They both had long legs and were gentle and easygoing. Their theme? Nautical chic! A sea theme was perfect for Willow.

As for me, I'd be walking with Frisco, of course. Skylar had assigned us a ladybug costume, so I was excited to don polka-dots with my fave four-legged friend. Things were really shaping up for the doggie fashion fundraiser.

"Who is my fashion buddy? I'm dying to know!" said Ashley.

"Ashley, you're going to be with Chicken!" said Skylar, pointing at the strange-looking mutt Willow and I had met at the shelter. I couldn't believe this odd pairing and was trying not to laugh. I noticed the other girls trying to hold back giggles as well.

"Are you sure you read that right?" Ashley asked with a frown.

"I sure did," Skylar replied with a smile.

Ashley looked a little taken aback, but she held it together well. I think she'd been picturing another fancy, adorable purse dog as her partner. The idea of girly-girl Ashley strutting up the runway with Chicken was too hilarious to handle!

In between giggles, Maren snuck a peek at Skylar's sheet. "Looks like you guys are going to have a Chia Pet theme," said Maren. "Now *this* should be entertaining!"

Even though Chicken wasn't exactly cover model material, Ashley wasn't one to be easily intimidated. I could already see her creative wheels turning. She scooped up Chicken and ruffled the tuft of hair on his head.

"You just wait, Chicken," she said. "I'll make you a star yet!"

Chicken must not have been feeling that idea, because he wriggled out of her grasp and sprinted down the grassy path toward the mall.

"Stop him!" yelled Skylar in a panic, but Chicken was a quick little beast. Skylar took off running after Chicken, as did Willow. Willow was one of the fastest runners in our class, so I knew if anyone could catch him, it would be her.

Willow and Skylar began darting between parked cars, trying to catch him. Ashley looked like she was going to cry, and I felt the same way. I prayed nothing awful would happen to Chicken! There were tons of cars coming in and out of the parking lot, and it was no place for a dog to be running around. I felt terrible that this had happened on my first day of work. This was *not* the impression I wanted to make.

Luckily, a friendly-looking old guy appeared a few minutes later holding a shaking Chicken. Skylar was right behind him.

"Found this little fella hiding under my car," he said. Skylar let out a dramatic sigh of relief. She grinned with gratitude as she took Chicken from him.

"Chicken, you scared us! Don't do that again!" she scolded him. He licked her nose in return.

An out-of-breath Willow appeared. "Is he okay?" she asked, between breaths. "I'm so glad you found him!"

"I'm so, so, so sorry!" Ashley said, near tears. "I was just trying to bond with him and instead I scared him away."

"It's okay," Skylar said. "You didn't do anything wrong. Chicken is easily spooked, and I should have told you that."

"Maybe I shouldn't be in the doggy fashion show," Ashley said sadly.

"Nonsense!" Skylar said. "From what I hear you bring fashion to life, and we need your help."

Ashley perked up after hearing that. "Thanks, Skylar."

"No, thank you for being willing to help," Skylar said.

It was hard to settle down and focus after all of the excitement, but the show must go on. The adoption had to get started. Plus, I think Ashley was more than ready to calm down with some retail therapy! I made a plan to meet the girls inside the mall afterward. After my friends left to shop, I turned my attention to Skylar.

"I'm not fired, right?" I asked, half-joking and half-serious. She shook her head and smiled.

"Of course not!" Skylar said. "These things happen. Let's get back to work."

"Thank goodness! Well, what do you need me to do?" I asked.

"The most helpful thing would be to help keep the water bowls full and welcome people who are interested in the animals," said Skylar. She handed me a digital camera. "Also, if you see the dogs doing something cute, snap a picture. We can post it on our blog."

It wasn't long before I had my first photo op! A family with a 4-year-old boy was playing with one of the chihuahuas. I managed to snap a shot of the chihuahua licking his face. Kodak moment, for sure. I also got a cool shot of a terrier chasing its tail — too cute.

Later, I got some video of a dog standing on his hind legs and dancing to the live mariachi band playing in the courtyard. One thing was for sure — this job definitely wasn't boring. It was actually a blast!

But the best moment of the day came when I met a girl around my age. Her name was Karissa. Like me, she'd been campaigning for a pet to call her own — except she wanted a cat. The good news? She'd succeeded! One of the Valley View volunteers had done a home check this past week, and her house had passed with flying colors. She and her dad were here to pick out her new feline friend.

I walked them over to the cat cages, where Skylar was helping a few other customers. Karissa immediately pointed to a beautiful cat with really bright blue eyes.

"Oh, she's so beautiful," she said. "I would recognize a Siamese cat anywhere, and that one is beyond gorgeous!"

I had been a big fan of Siamese cats ever since the first time I saw *Lady and the Tramp* as a little kid. "I totally agree," I said. "I think I read somewhere that it's actually the most popular breed in the U.S."

Skylar piped in and gave them some more information about what they could expect if they adopted a Siamese cat. Seeing the excitement in Karissa's eyes made me feel great. I loved matching pets with happy homes! Hopefully I'd know what that felt like someday soon, too.

chapter Seven

"Ah-*ha!*" called Ashley triumphantly, as she rummaged through one of the clearance bins. "I've found it! Chia perfection in a dress."

She held up a fuzzy, moss-green sheath dress that looked straight out of the 1960s. Holding it up to her body, she swooned, "Is this marvelously mod or what? I'm totally going to go try it on."

Thankfully, she'd moved past the Chicken disaster from earlier today. No shocker there, as shopping was known to improve her mood by leaps and bounds. Unfortunately, I wasn't having quite as much luck. We were rifling through the selections at Mayfair, one of the stores in the mall that had agreed to donate clothes for the fashion show. I hadn't found anything yet, but it was kind of fun shopping without having to think about spending my own money.

Willow tapped me on the shoulder. "Sorry to 'bug' you," she joked, making fake air quotes when she said the word "bug." "But I think I've found the ladybug look you're going for." She proudly showed me a bright red tulle skirt that had little black polka dots all over it. Kind of like a tutu, except longer and fluffier. Not my usual style, but I had to admit it definitely fit the bill!

"Well, that's original," came a voice from behind us.

"Yeah, if you're into the whole insect thing," said another voice. "Which would suit you since you bug everyone."

I didn't even need to turn around to know whose voices they were. I'd know those nasally tones anywhere — Franny and Zoey Martin. I swear they watched every teen movie ever made and tried as hard as they could to be the stereotypical mean girls. I will never understand it.

Maren stepped in. "It's a costume for a fashion show," she told them, crossing her arms in a "don't mess with us" stance. "We're trying to raise money for a good cause. I'm sure you probably can't relate to that, being pure evil and all."

Zoey batted her eyelashes. "Oh, well, why didn't you say it was for a fashion show?" she said. "We've done modeling before. Maybe you newbies need some talented twins to show you how it's done."

Ashley reappeared, wearing the green dress. "No, that won't be necessary," she said, sashaying between Franny and Zoey catwalk-style. We could always count on Ash to out-sass the Prickly Pair. "We've got the runway covered."

"Whatever," said Franny. "C'mon, Zoey, let's leave Ashley and her followers to play dress-up." They flounced off toward the juniors section. Those twins were too much!

Shortly afterward, an older saleswoman came up to see if we needed any help. Maren raised her eyebrows and grinned. I knew that mischievous look! Uh-oh.

"Actually, we're all good here," she said sweetly. "But, see those girls over there?" she asked, pointing at Franny and Zoey. As the saleswoman turned to look at Zoey and Franny, Maren grabbed grabbed two giant pairs of granny panties out of the bargain bin.

"They forgot these," she said with a serious look. "They mentioned it was really hard to find comfortable underwear, and I wouldn't want them to lose these."

We managed to hold in our laughter until the woman went over to Franny and Zoey, but we lost it once we saw their faces. They glared over at us with a poisonous look, and Ashley waved back innocently. The prickly princesses had been served!

Karma found its way back to us, though. We were at a kiosk looking at some cool glittery cell phone covers when Maren let out a yell.

"Why is my hair wet?" Maren yelled.

Seconds later, the same thing happened to Willow. "What in the world?" Willow said, feeling her wet hair.

Maren pointed to the upper level of the mall. "I think I spy the culprits," she grumbled. I followed her gaze, only to see Chase Davis and his buddy Noah Smith sporting a couple of giant squirt guns! Maren started running toward the escalator to track them down. "You guys are so dead . . ."

Watching her chase them around upstairs, I giggled to myself. When would these two just admit they liked each other? As if reading my mind, Ashley weighed in. "Maybe she just enjoys the thrill of the 'Chase,'" she joked.

While we were waiting for Maren to resurface, I heard my name being called. "Delaney!" It was Karissa and her dad, holding a pet carrier and a big bag of stuff from PetSmart.

"Look who's coming home with us." Karissa held up the carrier, and I peeked inside to see the pretty Siamese cat staring back. I clapped with glee.

"That's awesome, Karissa!" I said. "You're so lucky!"

"You can call me Rissa. That's what all of my friends call me," she answered. "And guess what I'm going to call her?" She gestured toward her new cat. "Joya."

"Aww, that's really unique," I told her. "You guys have to email us some photos once she gets settled. Maybe we can do a post on the rescue blog about it." I definitely had my thinking cap on. Skylar would be impressed.

Rissa nodded excitedly. "Yes, definitely!" she said. "Let's stay in touch." We exchanged phone numbers, and her dad even thanked me out for helping them earlier. It was a pretty good feeling.

When my mom and Gigi came to pick me up later, I was on cloud nine. My first day at the adoption event had gone really well (except for

Chicken pulling a vanishing act). Plus, I'd made a new friend, and we'd all had a blast shopping for the fashion show. But little did I know the best part of the day was yet to come — Karissa wasn't the only girl getting her wish.

"Mom, tell Laney!" Gigi bugged once we were in the car. She tugged on my mom's sleeve. "Tell her! Tell her!"

"Gigi, stop!" my mom said. She shook her head, laughing at Gigi's impatience. But my curiosity was tapped.

"What is it, Mom?" I asked. I was hopeful that I already knew the answer, but I didn't want to be disappointed.

She glanced over at me in the passenger seat and smiled. "Well, I wanted to wait until your dad and I were together to tell you, but I spoke to Skylar and we're going to foster Frisco next weekend," she said. "We thought it would work out well since the fashion show is on Sunday.

We can see how it goes over the weekend and take it from there."

I felt my heart almost burst out of my chest. I felt my mom's forehead jokingly. "Mom, are you okay? Do you have a fever? Have you gone temporarily insane?" I asked in disbelief.

But as it turned out, she was totally for real. "We're just really proud of the way you've gotten involved with the shelter. Dad and I think you're on the right road to being responsible enough," she said. "I'm not making any promises, but this is a start."

It was more than a start! It was a serious opportunity! No doubt Frisco was going to be the best house guest we'd ever had. And as his future owner and best friend, I was going to make sure next weekend went off without a hitch.

chapter Eight

Turns out getting the house ready for a pup (even if it's just for a few days) is a time-consuming task! Luckily, everyone was willing to help me. The week flew by as we prepared for Frisco's arrival. Ash did her part by lending me one of Coco's old cages. (Of course, she had "Frisco-fied" it by tying a blue bandanna around the edge and putting a fluffy blanket with a cursive "F" inside.) My dad found an old oversized beanbag pillow for Frisco to use as a dog bed, and my mom had helped me find some bowls to use for food and water.

Even Gigi got in the spirit. "Here, I got you something," she said, flopping on my bed after school one day. She handed me a gift, which was poorly wrapped but still thoughtful. I opened it up and found a blue-and-white striped leash.

"Aww, Geeg, that was sweet of you. Thanks girl," I said, giving her a little hug. (She wasn't *always* annoying.)

"I got it at the dollar store. Hope Frisco likes it!" she replied. "Maybe you'll even let me hang out with you guys at your sleepover, since I'm such a good sister?" Even though we shared a bedroom, the girls and I always slept in the family room. I had a strict "No little sisters allowed" policy. Gigi was always angling for a way in there. (Back to being annoying.)

"We'll see," I said. "Maybe, if you help me take care of Frisco."

Our Friday sleepover was moved to Saturday this week because of Frisco. Thankfully all of the girls were still able to come. (We didn't miss many Friday nights together, but an occasional tweak in our plans did happen.) Plus, the big doggie fashion show wasn't until Sunday, so it made more sense for all of us.

And when Friday rolled around, it was time for me and Gigi to live up to our promises. Gigi and I had a Junior Girl Scouts meeting after school, so my dad went to pick up Frisco at the shelter by himself. Usually I'm really into the meetings, but today I was super-antsy to just get through it and get home. I couldn't wait to hang with my furry friend!

My dad opened the front door once he saw us pull into the driveway. Guess who came flying out toward me? I bent down to give Frisco a big hug, and he started licking my face. This was the best greeting ever!

"My little buddy!" I exclaimed, laughing uncontrollably. "Oviously Frisco is happy to be here!"

Even my dad had to admit he was adorable. Once we brought him inside, it was kind of funny getting used to having Frisco around the house. He constantly followed me around, like, well, a puppy! I think he was probably just getting used to all of the new people, new smells, and his new surroundings. It made me happy that I was his familiar face. We already had a bond.

Before it got dark, Gigi and I took Frisco in the backyard to play. It was such a blast running around and playing fetch with him. Some of the volunteers had been teaching him commands like "sit" and "stay," so we helped him practice by giving him treats whenever he got it right. He wasn't totally trained yet, though. At one point, he started to dig up my mom's begonias.

Luckily, he stopped when I disciplined him, and my mom was a pretty good sport about it. (Whew! Close call.)

But my favorite part of the night was when my whole family sat down to watch a movie. My mom chose the classic dog movie *Beethoven* for the occasion, and Frisco curled up on my dad's makeshift dog bed. He seemed to be fitting into my family just fine! I sent some silent vibes toward my mom and dad that they would notice that, too.

Before we went to sleep that night, I laid down on the floor with Frisco. He seemed very content.

"You did such a good job today," I whispered. "I just know that you're meant to be part of the Brand family." I pulled out a treat I'd snuck into my pajama pocket. "Enjoy, boy!"

But in the morning, it turned out Frisco had a gift for me, too. I got out of bed, groggy and tired, and stepped in a fresh pile of dog poop on the floor!

"*Aghhh*," I screamed. "This was not what I signed up for!"

Gigi rolled over, still half-asleep. "Eww, gross!" she giggled, when she saw the mess. "I'll bring you a washcloth and get something to clean up the poop."

Frisco just stood in the corner, cowering a little bit. I felt bad. I'd probably scared him by yelling. Who knew if he was even house-trained? His old owners obviously hadn't taken good care of him and his family.

"It's okay, Frisco," I said, going over to pet him. "It's all good! We'll get you trained, don't you worry."

Gigi came back with a spray bottle of Resolve, some paper towels, and a soapy washcloth for me. After I cleaned my foot (so gross!), we managed to get everything back to normal again. Thank goodness for hardwood floors! Mom and Dad didn't need to know about this little snafu, right? No harm done.

The rest of the day, I got a little sneak preview of what my routine with Frisco would be like. It was hilarious watching him snarf down his food. Seriously, I think he wolfed it all within seconds!

Going on walks was fun, too. We even met a few of the other dogs that live on our block, like Greta the Great Dane and Joey D, a Corgi. I could barely wait until the girls came over later for the sleepover. My mom and dad had said we could take Frisco out for some fun. Dog park, here we come!

chapter Nine

The first one to arrive was Willow, and she had a surprise in tow. "Hey, Frisco!" she said, slinging her sleeping bag and stuff onto the couch. "I've got a little something for you." After rummaging through her bag for a bit, she pulled out a little box and handed it to me. "For you, m'lady."

I tore open the wrapping, and pulled out a cool dog collar Willow had made. She had taken a blue leather collar and bedazzled it with glittery studs.

I gave her a big hug. "Thanks, Wills," I told her. "Your gifts are always the best. Now Frisco can be fashionable long after the fashion show."

Ashley and Maren showed up not too long after. Both of them were dying to see Frisco, and *all* of us were more than ready for our sleepover after a long week at school. With the fashion show tomorrow, there was excitement and energy to spare!

Our plan was to head to the dog park before dinner, and apparently, it was Gigi's plan, too. "Can I come, Laney? Please, please, please?" begged Gigi. "It would be so much fun."

I shook my head. "No, this is just for us four," I said. "Maybe we can all hang out later. We'll play a game or something." I felt bad, but I didn't want my little sister tagging along. Sleepovers were *our* time for Maren, Willow, Ash, and me! Five was definitely a crowd.

My mom wasn't too impressed with my decision, though. "Delaney, there's no need to exclude your sister," she said sternly. "Gigi's been helping you with Frisco all weekend. She deserves a trip to the dog park, too." Gigi smiled in victory, and I had no choice but to relent. After all, she did help me clean up dog poop.

"Fine," I grumbled.

When we got to the dog park, lots of people were playing Frisbee with their pups or just letting them run free since the whole park was off-leash. The park was split up into a large dog and small dog area. I guess the division was made so that the dogs would feel more comfortable and not get scared. Since Frisco was around fifteen pounds, I wasn't sure which category he fell into?

Maren read my mind. "I bet Frisco can hang with the big dogs, D. All the ones in the small dog area are little Ashley-style frilly-willies. *Bo-ring*," she said, earning a "look" from Ashley. "No offense, Ash."

Sounded like good logic to me! I handed the leash to Gigi so I could take a swig from my water bottle. "Sounds good," I said, as we led Frisco inside the gate to the big dog area.

We found a great shady area, and Ashley set up our blanket under some trees. Willow got to work unpacking the mini-picnic basket my mom had made us, which was full of little treats like granola bars, string cheese, and homemade cookies. Oh, and dog treats for Frisco, of course.

Once the treats came out, we were suddenly the most popular people in the dog park. Frisco was in his element. He seemed to be hitting it off with a Greyhound named Cookie. They were wrestling around playfully.

"Go, Frisco!" joked Maren, egging them on. Cookie's owner, a college student named Eric, was pretty cool, too.

"How long have you had your Sheltie?" he asked me.

"Oh, actually I'm just fostering him," I answered. "He's one of the Valley View Rescue dogs. I'm hoping he'll be all mine soon, though!"

"Best thing you'll ever do," Eric said, looking at Cookie fondly.

"Oh, there he goes again!" I followed his gaze to see Cookie chasing Frisco in circles around the big lawn. I never knew Frisco could run so fast! They were really tearing it up. Fast friends, indeed.

Before I knew it, more dogs started joining in the fun, and suddenly there were eight dogs chasing Frisco! He was running in lightning-fast rings around the park. Everyone else was laughing at the spontaneous scene, but I suddenly got a little scared for him. Was this turning from playtime to a power struggle?

"Frisco! Time to come back!" I called, but he was out of earshot. The pack was hot on his heels!

When Frisco made it to the edge of the lawn, he jumped the fence and kept running into the woods! I was speechless. Eric and a couple of the other owners tried to assure me he couldn't have gone too far, but I was beside myself. This was *way* worse than when Chicken went missing. What if he didn't come back? Ash put her arm around me.

"Don't worry, Laney," she said. "He's probably just hiding behind a tree or something."

Take-charge Maren sprung to action. "Okay, Willow, come with me, we'll go into the woods and find him," she said. "Gigi and Ash, why don't you guys patrol the parking lot to make sure he doesn't escape? And Delaney, you stay here in case he comes back without any of us seeing him."

I gulped back tears. I felt like such a bad dog owner! "Okay, but hurry," I said. "My mom is going to pick us up soon!"

The time seemed to drag on while I waited for Maren and Willow to get back. A few of the other dog owners tried to make me feel better with stories of when their dogs had done similar things, but nothing seemed to help. And, sure enough, when they did come back, they were empty handed. No Frisco in sight!

I burst in tears. Sadly, parents were right. I wasn't ready for a dog. I was totally irresponsible. I should never have let Frisco in the big dog area.

"It's okay, Laney," said Willow. "You just know he'll turn up."

I wasn't so sure, and even worse, it was 5 p.m. Now it was time to face the music with my mom. She'd help us look for Frisco, but I was sure this was the nail in my dog-adopting coffin. We headed toward the parking lot, feeling defeated and worried.

"Over here, Laney!" I heard Gigi's voice. I looked over to see her, Ashley, and Frisco! They were standing outside my mom's car waiting for us. His tongue was wagging, and he seemed to have calmed down from all of the chaos. I ran up, feeling so relieved and ready to come clean to my mom.

But before I could explain anything, Gigi gave me a little wink. "Oh, yeah, I was just telling Mom how you'd stayed behind to clean up the picnic area," she said, nudging my side. "We were just telling her what a great time Frisco had today."

I raised my eyebrows, like "Are you serious?" But then I realized that she was trying to cover for me.

"It's definitely been a day to remember," I said, giving her a grateful look. Gigi could actually be pretty cool sometimes. I bent down to give Frisco the biggest hug ever. "And, now, we're ready to go home."

chapter Ten

I woke up on Sunday totally drained from what had happened at the dog park. It had been an emotional night, without a doubt. Feeling guilty, I'd come clean to my mom and dad about the dog park disaster. It just didn't feel right not to tell them. As expected, they weren't very happy about it, but they seemed to understand that it wasn't really my fault.

I wasn't really sure where things stood with adopting Frisco at this point, but I did know one thing: the show must go on! The day had finally come for the Valley View Rescue fashion show. The girls and I were holed up in my and Gigi's bedroom, getting runway ready, so to speak. Maren had even agreed to let Ashley do her hair (which was a miracle).

"What do you think?" I asked the girls, whirling around in my red tutu skirt. I'd paired it with a black short-sleeved leotard, a chunky red necklace, and a fun black antennae headband. My mom had said I could even wear some black eyeliner for the occasion. Score!

"Ladybuglicious," said Ash with a huge smile. Maren and Willow nodded in agreement, and Willow snapped a pic of me and Frisco for me to post on Facebook. Major "like!"

"You guys are the best. Seriously. Thanks for being so supportive," I told them, getting all emotional. "I don't know what I would have done without you yesterday — or any day for that matter."

Maren looked sheepish. "You probably could have done without my bad ideas," she apologized. "Next time, you make the call."

"No worries," I told her. "Frisco's over it, and so am I!"

By the time we made it over to the mall, things were already in full force. The rescue had set up a big tent, and lots of people were milling around waiting for a glimpse of the couture canines. I spotted Willow's family (including her twin, Winston) and Ashley's mom and dad, who'd already snagged seats in the crowd. Luckily, they'd saved some for my mom and dad and Gigi.

Backstage was a flurry of activity, and it was hilarious seeing all of the dogs dressed up in their costumes.

"Thanks for coming, girls," Skylar welcomed us. She seemed a bit frazzled, which was understandable. "You guys look great! Show starts in fifteen minutes sharp."

She pointed us over to another volunteer, who was arranging all of the models in a straight line in the order we'd be walking. Turned out Willow was second, and Maren was right after her! Ashley and I were assigned more toward the end. *Saving the best for last*, I thought, giving Frisco a fond look.

Sure enough, fifteen minutes later, the loud strains of "Who Let the Dogs Out?" came pounding over the loudspeaker. The crowd started clapping and cheering, and I felt a few butterflies flutter in my stomach. Willow looked nervous, too. She was more of a behind-the-scenes type, for sure. Unlike Ashley and Maren, who were totally revved up for their runway debuts.

"Welcome to the third annual Valley View Rescue fashion show! Who's ready to see some modeling mutts and support a great cause?" the MC yelled over the microphone. We could hear loud applause coming from the tent. "Okay, well, let's get started, then! First, let's meet Sheena and our exotic Italian greyhound, Marky Mark . . ."

Skylar motioned Sheena and Marky Mark through the curtain, and we could hear the crowd oohing and aahing at how cute they were. When she came back through the curtain, Sheena was all smiles. I relaxed a little. Maybe this was going to be fun.

"Anchors away!" boomed the announcer. "Next, let's welcome Willow and Hunter, our yellow Lab. He's four years old, great with kids, and he could use a lifeline. There are lots of fish in the sea, but only one dog just like this guy. Could he be *yours?*"

The script was a little cheesy, but it seemed to be doing its job. Willow and Hunter were a big hit with their nautical theme. Willow had striped leggings and a sailor hat. Plus, she'd found the cutest navy V-neck dress with a white anchor on the chest and a fun flare skirt. She'd tied a red scarf around her neck to top off the look. And, of course, Hunter looked equally adorable, with a striped shirt and a little life preserver around his neck.

Next up? Maren and Dig-Dug the Pug! Of course, in typical Maren form, she had truly gotten into character. She was rocking the caveman theme with this really cool leopard print suit. Her hair was in a high ponytail fastened together with a dog bone. She'd even painted some brown streaks across her cheeks! And Dig-Dug was a hoot, too. He had on a Viking hat and a little shield strapped to his back.

But even though their costumes were spot-on, Dig-Dug wasn't feeling the fashion show. Watching them try to go down the runway together was hilarious. Dig-Dug was moving really slowly and seemed to keep getting out of breath. He even laid down a few times!

"Aww, throw the little guy a bone," the announcer said to the audience, trying to get them to cheer for Dig-Dug. The crowd grew louder, and Maren was loving every minute of it. She scooped up Dig-Dug and sashayed down the rest of the runway, pumping her fist to get the crowd even more into it.

By the time it was Ashley's turn, everyone was having a blast. "Meet Ashley and Chicken. He's certainly one of a kind," said the announcer. "If you adopt this Chia pet, your love is sure to grow and grow."

The crowd went crazy for Ash's Chia dress and Chicken in his leafy green costume. The crowning moment was when Ash paused at the end of the runway and held a watering can over Chicken's head. Cuteness overload!

I was so caught up in the fun that I almost didn't notice my turn. "Go!" Skylar nudged me as she opened the curtain. I stepped through it, ready to walk down the long runway. Instead, off to the side, I saw my parents standing next to the announcer?!

Before I could react, the announcer motioned me and Frisco over. "This is one of our rescue's very special success stories," he told the crowd. "Delaney is in sixth grade at Valley View Middle School, and she's a new volunteer here at the rescue. As most volunteers do, Delaney fell in love with one of her dogs — our resident Sheltie, Frisco."

He paused as the crowd let out a collective "aww." "What Delaney doesn't know is that her parents have a surprise for her today," he continued, handing the mic to my dad. "Take it away!"

"Thank you. We've been very impressed by the rescue, and we want to help its cause," said my dad, smiling down at me and Frisco. "We're happy to welcome Frisco into our family full time!"

My parents gave me a huge hug, and the crowd cheered in approval. I was in shock! They'd totally faked me out! This fashion show finale was way better than any that I could have ever imagined. Frisco deserved a good home, and I couldn't believe that it was going to be ours! As the girls and the other volunteers came out with their dogs, I looked around and knew for sure that both Frisco and I were exactly where we belonged.

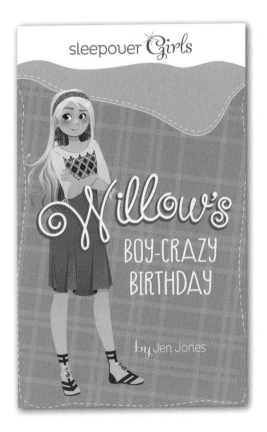

Can't get enough Sleepover Girls?
Check out the first chapter of

Willow's Boy-Crazy Birthday

chapter One

Twindom definitely has its perks — and pitfalls. Trust me, I should know. I'm one-half of Willow and Winston Keys (the double Ws). And, at the current moment, my beloved other half was both annoying me *and* also secretly helping me out. How? Well, he kept stepping on the backs of my moccasins, which was beyond irritating. But I didn't mind because one of his besties, Jacob Willis, had ended up walking home from school with us. And let's just say I wouldn't mind if Jacob was Winston's bestie and my boyfriend.

Thwap! Winston stepped on the back of my shoe again, and I tripped forward as my shoe came off. "Win!" I cried, grabbing it off the ground and hitting him with it. "Knock it off. Seriously."

He snatched the shoe back and threw it over to Jacob. "Pickle in the middle!" he yelled, throwing it back and forth with Jacob. I just stood there with my arms folded, blushing like a dork. It was just like Win to completely embarrass me in front of Jacob. Cute, dark-haired Jacob, rocking a casual style and black-rimmed glasses.

Luckily, my friend Ashley decided to step in and save the day. She swung her giant pink handbag in the air, blocking the shoe, and in a classic Ash move, it fell right into the purse!

"Game over, boys," she said, giving it back to me. "Here you go, Wills. And Win, really? Pickle in the middle? I didn't know we were five years old again."

I gave her a grateful look. If I could be one-tenth as confident as Ashley, I'd probably have a much better chance with Jacob. "I guess it's really true what they say about girls being way more mature than guys," I joked.

Winston made a face. "Is that why you still have your American Girl doll?" he teased me. I felt myself blush again and made a mental note to turn my American Girl doll into a voodoo doll with his name on it. Most of the time, we got along okay, but he was really on a roll today.

Instead of having a good comeback for him like usual, I felt totally tongue-tied in front of Jacob. (That was nothing new.) Thank goodness Ashley was always right there with a sassy saying, and once again, she didn't let me down. "Oh, so *that's* what I saw you playing with during Willow's last sleepover," she joked.

Jacob's ears perked up before Winston could retort. "Sleepover?" he asked. "Why wasn't I invited?"

Ashley pushed him playfully. "Maybe you should go look for that invite that got 'lost' in the mail."

I giggled. *That* invite wasn't going to happen anytime soon. As big of a crush as I had on Jacob, the idea of him crashing one of our sleepovers wasn't really that appealing. The reason was simple: our Friday night sleepovers were sacred girl time!

For about as long as I could remember, Ashley and I had been spending Friday nights with Delaney and Maren (and, lately, sometimes our new friend Sophie). Though we rotated houses, one thing was always the same: the ridiculous amount of fun that we had.

As for Winston, I had to hand it to him —
as annoying as he could be, he was usually a
pretty good sport when the fab four invaded
our household.

And, on that note, we'd arrived at our street,
which meant (sadly) saying *sayonara* to Ash and
Jacob. "See ya tomorrow, bro," said Winston.

"Later, guys," said Jacob. "I'll walk you home
the rest of the way, Ashley." Aww, spoken like
a true gentleman. Yet another reason to crush
on him.

Once they were out of sight and we were
headed down our street, I faced Winston
defiantly. "Why do you insist on torturing me?"
I asked, pouting.

A grin spread across Winston's face. "You
totally *like* Jacob, don't you?" he said. I shook
my head "no" quickly, but he wasn't having it.
"Willow loves Jacob, Willow loves Jacob," he
sang, over and over again.

"Will you *please* drop it?" I asked. I knew there was no use lying to him. We knew each other way too well. It was part of that whole twin thing. "If you don't, I'll tell Mom how you almost got detention the other day. Oh, and I guess that would mean getting grounded from video games again."

"Don't you dare," he said. "Race you home!" He took off with a head start up the hill, but I still managed to come in first as we breathlessly hit our driveway. Those long legs of mine did come in handy *sometimes*.

Being fraternal twins, I was actually a little bit taller than Winston; in fact, I was taller than almost all of the guys in our class. It was pretty awkward most of the time. (And don't even get me started on trying to find pants that aren't too short!)

Anyway, the simple act of arriving at home chilled me out a little. Even if I *weren't* a homebody (which I am), it'd be hard not to love our house. Our parents were all about being "one with nature," so they'd designed the house to be an indoor-outdoor oasis. One of my fave things about it was the glass atrium right in the center with a giant tree growing through it. The back of our house has floor-to-ceiling windows, which gives us a killer view of the valley. You could usually find me vegging out in my dad's recliner, listening to music and staring out the window.

But today my mom was sitting in my usual spot. She had two smoothies waiting for us as well. "Hey, Mom! You're home early," I exclaimed. My parents ran a health store called Creative Juices, so they had to work a lot.

"What can I say? I missed my terrific twosome," she said, handing us her newest smoothie creations. "Here, I made you guys pumpkin swirls." One of the tastier perks of having parents that ran a juice business was being a tester for the new creations.

"Thanks, Mom," said Winston, flopping onto the couch. "Did you put the vitamin B-12 shot in there this time? You always claim it helps concentration, so maybe it'll help me do better on my boring science homework."

She ruffled his hair. "You know it," she said. "Now you have no excuses." My parents were pretty strict with us about our schoolwork.

I took a sip and was rewarded with pumpkin-y goodness. "Yummmm!" I said, slurping up even more. "This is amazing!"

"Yep, it's October-rific," agreed Winston. He and I loved to come up with funny analogies for the way the juices and smoothies tasted.

"You are correct, brother," I said with a fake accent. "It's like autumn in a glass."

"Why yes, sweet sister," he responded. "It most definitely is. A pumpkin patch of goodness."

My mom grinned. "Well, actually, that was what I wanted to talk to you two about," she said. "It's practically Halloween, and we still haven't talked about what we're going to do for your birthdays."

Birthdays were a big deal in our house — after all, there was double the reason to celebrate! Usually, Winston and his friends went out and did something like mini-golf or paintball, but I tended to stick with the tried-and-true: a sleepover with my besties. However, I usually get to have a two-night sleepover for my birthday, which is extra special. Plus, we always did another party with our extended family.

"Yeah, we'll have to pick a date for the two-night sleepover," I agreed. I was already mentally planning which chick flicks to watch. And maybe we could do pumpkin carving! I'd already been painting a bunch of pumpkins and putting them out on the front porch. Art was my favorite thing in the whole world, and I always had something creative happening.

My mom looked thoughtful. "Well, actually, your Dad and I thought this year you two could have a co-ed birthday party," she suggested. "It might be fun to invite a bunch of your classmates and do a big Halloween costume party. Plus, it would make things a lot easier on your dad and me to do both parties at once."

Winston lit up at the thought. "Are you kidding me?" he said. "That would be awesome!"

That was easy for him to say — he was totally outgoing. As for me, aka "the shy one," I wasn't sure how to feel. Being the center of attention always made me uneasy, and having a big party was very, well, un-me. On the other hand, I knew Ashley, Maren, and Delaney would be super-jazzed to help me plan, and there was always the Jacob factor, which was a huge bonus! And it was about time I tried to get out of my social comfort zone, or at least that's what I kept telling myself.

So that left just three words for my verdict: "Count me in."

Which Sleepover Girl Style Fits You – Delaney, Maren, Willow, or Ashley?

1. What is your favorite color?
   a) green
   b) orange
   c) blue
   d) purple

2. What kind of pajamas do you like?
   a) oversized jersey
   b) tank top and yoga pants
   c) T-shirt and shorts
   d) nightgown

3. What did you wear on the first day of school?
   a) a comfy hoodie and jeans
   b) animal print sweater and capris
   c) tunic and leggings
   d) sparkly tank, cardigan, and skirt

4. What is your ideal hair style?
   a) curly and loose
   b) simple ponytail
   c) straight and long
   d) short and stylish

5. What is your purse style?
   a) no purse — just a backpack
   b) cross-body bag
   c) oversized tote
   d) a clutch

6. What is your favorite accessory?
   a) ponytail holder
   b) charm bracelet
   c) chunky necklace
   d) anything sparkly

7. What is your favorite store?
   a) Target
   b) PetSmart
   c) Michaels
   d) Old Navy

8. What is your favorite print?
   a) no print
   b) animal
   c) flowers
   d) polka dots

9. What type of shoes do you prefer?
   a) tennis shoes
   b) ballet flats
   c) sandals
   d) boots

Got mostly "a" answers? You are Maren.
Got mostly "b" answers? You are Delaney.
Got mostly "c" answers? You are Willow.
Got mostly "d" answers? You are Ashley.

Want to throw a sleepover party your friends will never forget?

Let the Sleepover Girls help!
The Sleepover Girls Craft titles
are filled with easy recipes, crafts,
and other how-tos combined with
step-by-step instructions and colorful
photos that will help you throw the
best sleepover party ever! Grab all
four of the Sleepover Girls Craft titles
before your next party so you can create
unforgettable memories.

About the Author
Jen Jones

Using her past experience as a
writer for E! Online, Jen Jones has
written more than forty books about
celebrities, crafting, cheerleading,
fashion, and just about any other
obsession a girl in middle school
could have — including her popular
Team Cheer! series for Capstone.
Jen lives in Los Angeles.